THE HEIGHTS

SWAMP

SADDLEBACK
EDUCATIONAL PUBLISHING

T H E   H E I G H T S

Blizzard	River
Camp	Sail
Crash	Score
Dive	**Swamp**
Neptune	Twister

Original text by Ed Hansen
Adapted by Mary Kate Doman

SADDLEBACK
EDUCATIONAL PUBLISHING
www.sdlback.com

ISBN-13: 978-1-61651-625-3
ISBN-10: 1-61651-625-9
eBook: 978-1-61247-310-9

Printed in Guangzhou, China
0611/CA21100644

16 15 14 13 12   1 2 3 4 5 6

Chapter 1

The sky was gray. It was going to rain soon. Jake Woods didn't want to go outside. But he didn't have a choice. Jake was in jail. And he had work duty. He had to go outside.

Jake lined up for the prison bus. He was on trash detail. All the men wore orange jumpsuits. They all looked alike.

Jake sat alone. He looked out the

window. He had just turned 21. And his life was a mess. He hadn't done anything too bad. Not bad enough to be in jail.

Jake's father left. Jake dropped out of school. Jake started stealing animals in the Everglades. Alligators sold for $200 on the black market.

This was illegal. But he made a living. Because he knew the swamp, Jake was good at stealing.

But Jake didn't get arrested for stealing. He was in jail for something he didn't do. He was innocent.

The trouble started one night. Jake stopped in a store for bread. It was 3 o'clock in the morning. Jake had been out stealing. The store was empty. A clerk was behind the counter. He read the newspaper.

Jake went to the back of the store. He got the bread. As he turned around he saw Rip Poole. Rip wasn't a good friend. But Jake knew him. Rip was a bad guy.

"Hey, Rip, what's going on?" Jake asked.

Rip smiled. But Jake thought he looked strange.

"Nothing, yet," Rip answered.

Jake turned around. He walked to the counter. Rip followed him. Jake put the bread on the counter.

Rip pulled out a gun! He pointed it at the clerk.

"Open the cash register! Make it fast!" Rip yelled.

Jake was shocked.

"Put the gun away, Rip!" Jake yelled. "What are you doing?"

"Shut up, Jake!" was all Rip said.

The clerk froze. Then he stepped on a silent alarm. The silent alarm called the police.

"I can't open the drawer," the clerk said.

"Come on, Rip. Stop this!" Jake yelled.

"I told you to shut up!" yelled Rip.

Then Rip grabbed the clerk by the shirt. He pushed the gun into his chest.

"Get the money now!" Rip ordered.

The clerk opened the cash drawer. Rip jumped over the counter. He pushed the clerk aside. He grabbed the money. Just then, two police cars pulled up.

Jake and Rip saw the flashing lights. Rip was mad.

"You called the cops!" yelled Rip.

Then Rip raised the gun. He pointed it at the clerk. Then he fired.

Two police officers ran into the store.

"Don't shoot!" Jake yelled.

He raised his hands. Rip ran out the back door. But two more officers were waiting for him. They told Rip to drop his gun. He didn't drop it. He shot at the officers. They shot back. Rip fell to the ground. He was dead.

The police arrested Jake. They didn't believe his story. Jake was a known thief. They thought he was with Rip. The clerk couldn't help him. He was in a coma. The EMT said he wouldn't last the night.

Jake was sentenced to 20 years. The court thought Jake aided in an armed robbery. That made him as guilty as Rip. At the time, Jake was only 18.

Three years passed. Jake knew he couldn't last 17 more years. He thought of all kinds of escape plans. But only one made sense. Jake knew the Everglades very well. All he had to do was get close. Then he could run. They'd never find him.

Rafael and Ana sat on the beach. They watched Antonio and Lilia play in the ocean. Franco was with his friends for spring break this year.

It was the third day of their vacation in Florida. But Rafael was bored.

"Aren't you tired of just sitting on the beach?" Rafael asked.

"No," answered Ana. "It's great. But I know you're tired of the beach. This is just like being in the Heights. Only warmer. What do you want to do?"

"How about taking an airboat ride in the Everglades? It should be a lot of fun," Rafael said.

"Go find out more about it," said Ana.

Rafael made a few calls. Alvarez Airboat Tours had an opening the next day. Rafael booked the tour.

"Don't worry about lunch. It's included. I'll bring lunch for you and your family. See you tomorrow morning, 8 o'clock," Chris Alvarez said.

At dinner, Rafael told Lilia and Antonio about the airboat. They were both excited.

"Will we see any alligators?" Antonio asked.

"I think we will," said Rafael. "There are a lot of them in the Everglades. We have to get up very early tomorrow. It's an hour away. It's an all-day trip!"

Ana smiled at her family. She knew her kids and Rafael couldn't wait! They loved adventure. She liked to relax. That's why she liked the Heights. A Silva family adventure often went to pieces.

Chapter 2

Jake Woods got out of bed. He was in a bad mood. Every day was the same in jail. Today would be different for Jake. But he didn't know that yet.

Jake boarded the prison bus. Time for work detail. He closed his eyes. And he tried to sleep. A guard woke him up an hour later.

Jake knew exactly where he

was. This was the swamp where he caught alligators.

His mind was racing. They were on the edge of the Everglades. He was sure he could escape.

It was close to noon. Jake moved to the edge of the swamp. The guards weren't watching him. He ran into the swamp.

Jake ran deep into the swamp. Soon he heard a lot of noise. The guards discovered he was missing!

A lot of people would be looking for him. Jake had to get out of his orange jumpsuit.

Jake remembered a small marina. He could steal an airboat. Jake ran toward Alvarez's Airboat Tours.

He ran to the swamp. The water

was deep. The air was hot. He was sweating.

It was dangerous in the Everglades. There were alligators and snakes. But Jake wasn't afraid of them. He was afraid of getting caught.

Jake watched Chris Alvarez fill up his boat with gas. He swam to the dock. Then got out of the water. Chris didn't hear him. Jake picked up a hammer. He wrapped it in a rag. Then he slammed it down on Chris's head.

Jake dragged Chris to the boathouse. Then he changed into Chris's clothes. He tied him up with strong rope. He gagged him.

Tomorrow's date was circled on

Chris's calendar. It read: *8 a.m., day tour—the Silva family.*

"What a great cover!" Jake thought. "I'll pretend to be Chris Alvarez. I'll take the Silvas on a tour of the Everglades."

Jake found a small gun in a drawer. It was loaded. He put the gun in his pocket. All he had to do was wait for the Silvas.

Chapter 3

The Silvas were late for the airboat trip. They ran down the dock to meet Chris.

"Good morning. You must be Chris," said Rafael. "I'm sorry we're late. We ran into a police roadblock."

"Wow! What was it for?" Jake asked.

"Someone escaped from prison. There's a big manhunt," said Rafael.

Jake's mind was racing. He needed to get into the swamp.

"Well, I hope they catch him. Now let's go!" Jake said.

Everyone got on the boat. And they were off!

Jake headed into the swamp. He drove fast. The airboat scared a lot of birds. The Silvas couldn't see much.

"Why is he going so fast?" asked Ana. "We'd see more if he'd slow down."

Rafael tapped Jake on the arm.

"Let's slow down. We want to see more of the swamp," said Rafael.

"We'll be at a preserve soon. There are a lot of animals there. I'll slow down then," Jake said.

Rafael wasn't happy. But he

listened to Jake. The airboat raced through the Everglades. It was getting close to noon.

"Stop the boat, Jake," Rafael yelled. "We need to talk."

Jake stopped the boat. He looked at Rafael.

"We're hungry. We'll eat lunch. Then I want you to slow down. Where's the food?" Rafael asked.

"I don't have any food," Jake answered. "Why didn't you bring your own lunch?"

Rafael knew something was wrong.

"You aren't Chris Alvarez, are you?" asked Rafael.

"No, Mr. Silva. I'm not," Jake answered. Then he pulled the gun from his pocket. "I don't want to hurt anyone. Do as you're told. I'll be gone soon. Then you can have this boat."

"Oh, no, Rafael!" Ana said. "He's the convict who escaped yesterday!"

Jake nodded his head. Then he started the boat again.

Rafael took a deep breath. Then he jumped on Jake. The two men struggled. Ana tried to grab the controls. But she lost her balance. She was thrown into the swamp.

The boat hit a tree. It flipped over. Rafael, Jake, and Lilia were thrown into the water. The airboat was a total wreck!

Lilia and Ana swam to shore. They weren't hurt. Rafael dragged Jake to the shore. He knew Jake wasn't a threat. He'd lost his gun in the struggle.

"Where's Antonio?" Lilia cried.

"Antonio! Antonio!" Rafael yelled.

"Over here, Dad!" Antonio yelled back. "I'm stuck in the boat!"

Antonio was trapped in the wrecked airboat. He wasn't hurt. But it would take a long time to free him.

Chapter 4

Jake sat on the edge of the swamp. He thought about running. The Silvas were trying to free their son. They weren't watching him.

But Antonio was in more danger than the Silvas knew. Jake tried to forget it. "Come on, Jake, get moving," he said to himself.

But Jake couldn't run. It was his fault Antonio was trapped. "I can't

let the kid die here," Jake thought.
Jake went back into the water.

"Mr. Silva?" said Jake.

"What are you still doing here?" Rafael snapped.

"This is my fault. I want to help get your son free," answered Jake.

"You've done enough. I don't need your help," Rafael snarled.

"Yes, you do. There are tides in this part of the swamp. In another 30 minutes, we'll be underwater," Jake said.

Rafael was stunned. He knew Jake was right. Rafael saw the high-water marks on the trees. At high tide, Antonio would drown!

"Can we free him in 30 minutes?" asked Rafael.

"Maybe not. But two of us can work faster," said Jake.

Rafael and Jake tried to pull Antonio out. He was really stuck. Ana was scared. She watched the water rising.

"It's no use!" Rafael yelled. "We'll never free him!"

Antonio fought to keep his head above water. He only had a few breaths left.

Jake asked Rafael for a knife. Rafael didn't want to give a knife to a criminal. But he had no choice.

Jake went under the water. He came up holding a tube. He had cut the tube from the engine. Rafael was amazed.

"Breathe through this tube, kid.

We'll get you free. Relax. You can do it," Jake said. "Mrs. Silva, hold the other end of this tube above the water."

Rafael and Jake went back to work. The wreck was bad. Jake remembered there was a toolbox on the boat. There was a saw in it. He dove down to find it. It took him five tries to find it.

Jake sawed through the metal. It took a long time, but he made a hole. Antonio swam through.

"You saved my son's life. I can't thank you enough. What's your name?" asked Rafael.

"It's Jake—Jake Woods. And I'm really sorry for all this trouble. It's my fault," Jake said.

"Well, Jake," said Rafael. "You sure made up for it. You could've left. Why did you help us?"

"I don't really know," Jake said. "I didn't want Antonio's death to be my fault."

Jake told them about the robbery. He said no one believed that he was innocent.

The Silvas believed him. There was something good about Jake. Rafael and Ana had the same thought. Jake shouldn't be in jail.

Chapter 5

"You know," Jake said. "We're five miles from the edge of the swamp. If we leave now, we can get out before dark."

"What are you going to do, Jake?" Rafael asked.

"Keep on running, I guess," Jake answered. "If I turn myself in, I'll go back to prison."

"But what if we can get your case reopened. With a good lawyer...

I can't promise anything. But it's worth a try," Rafael said.

"I don't have any money. I can't get a good lawyer," Jake said. "And even if I could, I don't know one. I can't prove that I wasn't helping Rip. Who would believe me?"

"I believe you," Rafael answered. "And I know a lawyer in Miami. He's a good friend. I'll talk to him about your case."

Jake thought about Rafael's offer. No one had ever been so nice to him.

Lilia was bored. She was sick of sitting in a swamp. There was a pile of dirt by the water. Lilia walked over to it.

"Lilia," Jake yelled. "Get away from there!"

Everyone watched as a huge alligator came out of the water. It looked right at Lilia. Jake ran over. He pulled Lilia away. The alligator stopped when it saw Lilia move.

"That dirt pile is an alligator nest," explained Jake. "Her eggs are in there."

Everyone moved far away from the nest. They watched the alligator go back into the water.

They started walking through the swamp.

"Have you made up your mind, Jake?" Rafael asked. "What are you going to do?"

"Do you really think I have a chance?" Jake asked.

"There's always a chance. And any

chance is better than no chance," said Rafael. "I don't think you want to live as a fugitive. You're too good for that."

The Silvas and Jake finally made it out of the swamp. Jake led everyone to a little restaurant. No one had eaten that day. They were all hungry. Everyone had two burgers except Jake and Antonio. They had three!

"I thought about what you said, Mr. Silva. I don't want to be a fugitive," said Jake. "I'm going to turn myself in."

Jake asked Rafael to call the police. They came very fast. They took Jake back to jail.

Everyone was tired. They'd had a very long day!

Chapter 6

The next morning, Rafael got up
early. He called his friend Jorge
Cruz. Jorge had a good law practice
in Miami. He was also Rafael's dive
partner. Franco and Rafael went
scuba diving on his boat. Rafael
knew Jorge could help Jake. They
planned to meet for lunch.

Jorge was at the restaurant when
Rafael arrived. They shook hands.

"What do you need help with, Rafael?" asked Jorge.

"I don't need your help. But a young man I met does," said Rafael.

Rafael told Jorge about Jake.

"Wait," Jorge said. "You want to help a guy who kidnapped your family? And knocked Alvarez out cold? And stole a gun?"

"He saved Antonio's life," answered Rafael.

"But he was the one who put Antonio in danger," Jorge said.

"I know that. But he could have run. And he didn't. He's not bad," Rafael said.

"You don't know this guy. He could be lying," Jorge said. "He can't even prove he's innocent."

"I believe him, Jorge. I have a feeling. He shouldn't be in jail for the robbery. Do you think you can help?" asked Rafael.

"Okay, I'll help," Jorge said. "But not for free. I'll charge the minimum. It will be expensive. It costs a lot of money to reopen cases. I'll see what I can do.

"Jake will pay back every penny," said Rafael. "I'll back up the debt."

"I'll look into the case. I'll try and keep the cost down," said Jorge. "I'll let you know what I find out."

Chapter 7

Rafael hadn't talked to Jake in weeks.
He wondered how he was doing.
Rafael also wondered how Jorge was
doing. He wanted to call him. But he
knew Jorge would call when he had
news. The case wasn't easy.

Jorge called the next day.

"I've got some good news," Jorge
said. "I talked with the clerk who got
shot. He's fully recovered now. His

memory is better. He told me Jake came in the store after Rip Poole. He also said Jake didn't have a gun. He doesn't even think Jake was involved."

"That's great!" Rafael said.

"There's more good news. There was another customer in the store that night. She didn't testify before."

"You're kidding," Rafael answered.

"No," Jorge said. "An old lady saw everything. She saw Rip pull the gun. Then she hid. I talked to her yesterday. She wants to help Jake. She'll testify that Jake tried to stop the robbery."

"That's wonderful!" Rafael cried out.

"We can get the court to reopen

Jake's case," Jorge said.

"Why didn't the police know this before?" asked Rafael.

"I don't know. But it does happen sometimes," Jorge said.

"Anything else?" asked Rafael.

"Well, it would help Jake's case if he paid Chris Alvarez. Chris lost his boat. It would make Jake look good. The judge would approve," Jorge said.

Rafael put the phone down. He thought about what Jorge said. Jorge did a lot to help Jake. And Rafael had always felt bad for Chris Alvarez. They did crash his airboat. And airboats cost money. Jake should help Chris get a new airboat.

Rafael called Jake. He couldn't

believe the news. He'd never been so happy. Jake agreed to help Chris. And he agreed to repay Rafael.

Rafael bought Chris a new airboat. Jake would pay Rafael back when he was out of jail. He would also pay Jorge's fees. Every month he would send the Silva's a check.

Chapter 8

Jorge got Jake's case reopened. Jake wasn't guilty. Jorge wanted to get him out of jail.

Rafael and Ana went to Miami. They wanted to support Jake in court. The case was strong. Jorge told Jake's side of the story. He said Jake wasn't with Rip. Jake had no plans to rob the store. He was there to buy bread. The clerk and the other

customer were ready to testify. They
didn't think Jake was part of the
robbery.

The trial ended quickly. The
evidence proved that Jake was not
guilty. The surprise witness was
Elsa Flores.

"That young man tried to stop the
robbery," Elsa said.

The district attorney questioned
Mrs. Flores. He wanted to know
why she was in the store so late. He
also wanted to know why she didn't
testify earlier. She told the court
she liked to shop when the store
was empty. She didn't testify before
because the police never asked her.

But the best witness was the
clerk. He stated that Jake was not

with Rip.

"Jake Woods didn't rob the store. He tried to stop Rip," said the clerk.

The jury cleared Jake. He was a free man!

Rafael and Ana took Jake out to dinner to celebrate.

"What are you going to do now?" asked Rafael.

"First I need a job. And I want to get my high school diploma. Dropping out of high school was stupid. I know that now," said Jake.

"I have a lot of friends in construction. I can get you a job. But only if you'll work hard," Rafael said.

"Oh, Mr. Silva! That would be awesome!" Jake exclaimed. "I

promise I'll work very hard!"

Now that Jake was free there were a lot of changes in his life. Rafael got him a job in construction. He brought home a good salary. Each month Jake sent a check to Rafael. Jake also signed up for night classes. He was working toward his GED.

After three years behind bars, Jake's life was good again.

Chapter 9

It was early in December. Snow was falling in Rockdale Heights. Rafael and Ana enjoyed a nice Saturday. Franco was at college. Antonio and Lilia were outside.

"I have an idea," said Ana. "Why don't we invite Jake to come up for Christmas? He can finally Meet Franco."

"That's a great idea!" Rafael

said. "He's been working so hard. A vacation would be good for him."

Rafael called Jake. He asked Jake if he'd like to come for Christmas.

"I'd love to!" Jake said. "I've never been out of Florida."

Ana told Antonio and Lilia that Jake was coming.

"That's cool!" said Lilia. "I like Jake."

"You *should* like him," Antonio said. "If it wasn't for Jake, you'd have been alligator food!"

"I feel bad Jake was in jail so long. How did the court make such a big mistake?" Lilia asked.

"Sometimes bad things happen. Jake was in the wrong place. It looked like he was guilty. He never got a fair chance," Rafael answered.

"I'm glad his life is better now," Lilia said. "He seems to be doing great."

Jake was doing great. It was a good thing he met the Silvas!

Chapter 10

It would have been easy to walk
away from Jake. But Rafael was glad
he didn't. He felt good about helping
him. And he was proud that Jake
was working so hard.

It was two days before Christmas.
Rafael picked up Jake from the
airport. Jake looked older. He looked
happier.

"Hi, Jake!" said Rafael. "Welcome to Rockdale Heights!"

"Thanks again, Mr. Silva." Jake said. "You've done so much for me. I still can't believe this is my life!"

The rest of the Silvas were at the house. Jake finally met Franco. They spent the day talking about football.

Antonio and Lilia took Jake ice skating. He'd never been on skates. He'd never even seen snow! Jake spent a lot of time sitting on the ice. Lilia and Antonio laughed when Jake fell.

"Keep trying, Jake," Lilia shouted. "You'll get it!"

"By the time I get it, I'll be too sore to walk!" said Jake.

They had a great time. Jake had

always been alone. He never had a family. Now he was one of the Silvas.

Everyone enjoyed Christmas. Ana made a big dinner. Everyone opened gifts. It was a wonderful day.

Jake had a surprise for Rafael. He had paid him back for the airboat. But he wanted to do something special.

"I know I paid you back for Chris's airboat. But I still felt bad that I crashed it. And I feel bad that I hit him. So I went to apologize in person. And we became friends."

"That's wonderful," Rafael said. "I'm glad you're making new friends."

"Chris and I started talking about the Everglades. He knows a lot about boats. But he doesn't know much about the swamp. Chris wants me to be a tour guide. I start next week!" Jake said.

The Silvas were so happy for Jake. He found a job that he loved. And that he was good at.

"I'm paying Jorge back. But I'm also saving up for my own airboat. We'll double Chris's business," said Jake. "I'm naming the boat Silva. I want you to take the first tour. You never did get to tour the Everglades."

"That's because you were going too fast!" Antonio said.

"At least I got to see an alligator up close!" said Lilia.

I am *so* glad that I wasn't there!" said Franco.

Everyone laughed. They enjoyed the rest of their time together. Then Jake returned to Florida. The holidays were over.

A few months later, the Silva family went to Florida again for Spring Break. They toured the Everglades. And Jake was their guide.

Rafael looked at Jake. He was back working in the Everglades. This time it was legal. Jake really came a long way from his prison cell. And it was all because of the Silvas.